Sesame Street Start-to-Read Books™
help young children take a giant step into reading.
The stories have been skillfully written, designed,
and illustrated to provide funny, satisfying
reading experiences for the child just starting out.
Let Big Bird, Bert and Ernie, Oscar the Grouch,
and all the Sesame Street Muppets get your child
into reading early with these wonderful stories!

Library of Congress Cataloging-in-Publication Data:
Hautzig, Deborah. Why are you so mean to me? (A Sesame Street start-to-read book) SUMMARY: When his schoolmates laugh at him for not being able to hit the ball in a baseball game, Grover is so upset that he is mean to his friend Big Bird. [1. Behavior—Fiction. 2. Friendship—Fiction. 3. Puppets—Fiction] I. Cooke, Tom, ill. II. Henson, Jim. III. Children's Television Workshop. IV. Title. V. Series: Sesame Street start-to-read books.   PZ7.H2888Wh   1986   [E]   85-18434
ISBN: 0-394-88060-9 (trade); 0-394-98060-3 (lib. bdg.)
Manufactured in the United States of America   1 2 3 4 5 6 7 8 9 0

Why Are You So MEAN TO ME?

by Deborah Hautzig • illustrated by Tom Cooke

Featuring Jim Henson's Sesame Street Muppets

Random House/Children's Television Workshop

Why Are You So MEAN TO ME?

by Deborah Hautzig • illustrated by Tom Cooke

Featuring Jim Henson's Sesame Street Muppets

Random House/Children's Television Workshop

Grover woke up smiling.
Today was the day
of the school picnic
in Bluebird Park!

His mother gave Grover
a big picnic lunch.
Then she said,
"I have a surprise for you."

It was a baseball bat!
Grover was so happy.
"Now you can learn to play baseball,"
said his mother.
"I will be a super batter,"
said Grover.
Grover's mother gave him
a big kiss good-bye.

The school bus took everyone
to Bluebird Park.
Grover sat in the back
with Truman.

"My big brother has a bat
just like yours.
I play ball with him
all the time," said Truman.
"I have never played before,"
said Grover.
"I cannot wait to try!"

There was so much to do
at the park!
Everyone played tag.

Betty Lou showed Grover
a new trick
on the monkey bars.

Then there was a sack race.

At noon they had
their picnic lunch.

After lunch it was time
to play baseball.
The teacher said, "Jill and Truman,
you pick two teams."

One by one everyone was picked.
Everyone but Grover.

"Truman, you need one more,"
said the teacher. "Take Grover."
Truman said, "Oh, no!
Grover has never played before.
He will make us lose!"
Truman's words hurt Grover.
They felt like a punch.
But Grover just said,
"You will see.
I will be a super batter!"

But Grover was not a super batter.

He missed the ball every time.

Now was his last chance.

He swung three times . . .

and he missed three times.

The other team shouted, "We won!"

"See? I told you
  Grover is no good," said Truman.
  Everyone laughed.
"Grover can't bat!" they teased.
  Grover pretended not to hear.
  But he felt very sad.

Grover walked home very slowly
from the bus stop.
"Why did all my friends
make fun of me?"
he said to himself.
A big tear rolled down
his furry face.

He kicked a tin can
down the street.
"You stupid can," he said.
Then he looked at his bat.
"You stupid bat!" he said.

When Grover came to Oscar's
trash can, he bumped into Big Bird.
"Hi, Grover!" said Big Bird.
"Look! Oscar gave me
this blue paint.
I am painting a picture of you!"

Grover looked at the picture.

"That stinks!" he yelled.

"That does not look

like me at all!"

Big Bird's eyes filled with tears.

"Grover, why are you

so mean to me?" said Big Bird.

"I am your FRIEND!"

Oscar popped out of his can.
"Who is making all that noise?"
he yelled.
"Big Bird is!" said Grover.
"Grover is!" said Big Bird.

Grover looked at Oscar.
He looked at Big Bird.
Then he burst into tears.
"Everyone made fun of me."
And he told them all about
the baseball game.

"Poor Grover!" said Big Bird.

"You must feel so sad."

Oscar yelled, "SAD?

You must mean MAD!"

Grover said, "I am sad AND mad."

Then he began to smile a little.

Big Bird said,

"I have a good idea.

I will practice batting with you."

Oscar gave them

a rotten old ball.

"Now GO AWAY!" he said.

Big Bird threw the ball to Grover
again and again.
At last Grover hit the ball.
"Hurray!" said Big Bird.

Then Grover threw the ball
to Big Bird again and again.
Big Bird missed every time.

"I am even worse than you,"
said Big Bird.
Grover and Big Bird
laughed and laughed.

Finally it was time to go home.
"Big Bird," Grover said softly,
"I did not mean it
when I said
your painting stinks.
Please, may I have it?"
Big Bird's face lit up.
"Sure you can!" said Big Bird.
Grover said, "I will go home
and hang it up right now."
He ran all the way.

"Hello, dear!" said his mother.
"Did you have fun at the picnic?"
  Grover said, "Some of it was fun.
  But then everyone made fun of me
  because I was a bad batter."
"Oh, my goodness," said his mother.
"What did you do?"
  Grover said,
"I yelled at Big Bird.
  Then I felt worse!"

"Oh, my," said his mother.

"Then what?"

Grover said, "Then we played
and Big Bird gave me
this nice painting."

His mother said,

"Big Bird is a good friend."

Grover's mother helped him
hang up Big Bird's painting.
Then they had a nice hot supper.

After supper Grover said,
"Mommy, will I EVER be
good at batting?"
His mother said, "Maybe you will
when you are older...
and maybe you will not."
Then she smiled.
"But you will ALWAYS
be good at being Grover.
And that is even better."